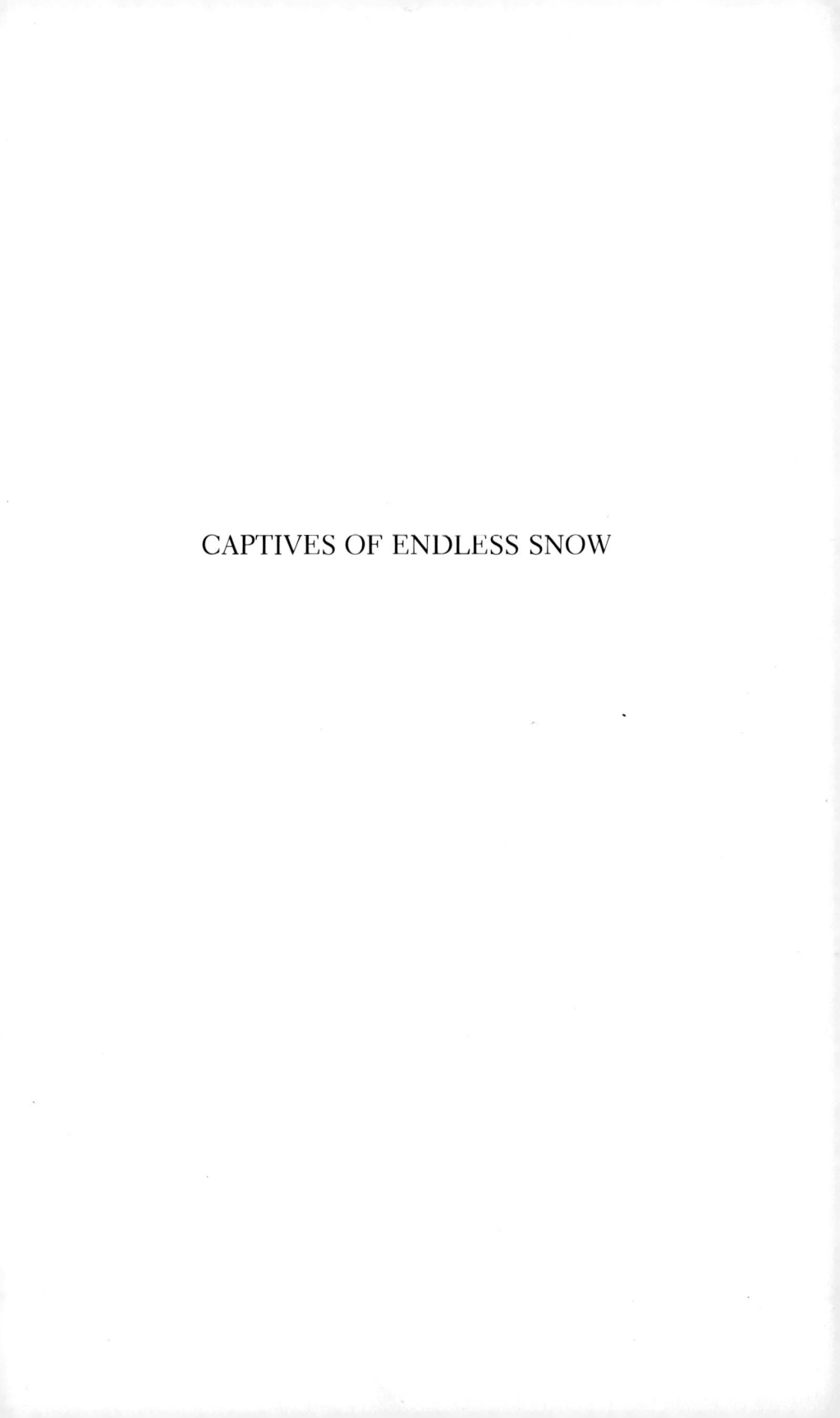

CAPTIVES OF ENDLESS SNOW

CAPTIVES OF ENDLESS SNOW

Priscilla Turner
Illustrated by Tony Baldini

RAINTREE PUBLISHERS
Milwaukee • Toronto • Melbourne • London

Copyright © 1980, Raintree Publishers Inc.

All rights reserved. No part of this book may be reproduced or utilized in any form or by any means, electronic or mechanical, including photocopying, recording, or by any information storage and retrieval system, without permission in writing from the Publisher. Inquiries should be addressed to Raintree Publishers Inc., 205 West Highland Avenue, Milwaukee, Wisconsin 53203.

Library of Congress Number: 79-22194

1 2 3 4 5 6 7 8 9 0 84 83 82 81 80

Printed and bound in the United States of America.

Library of Congress Cataloging in Publication Data

Turner, Priscilla.
  Captives of Endless Snow.

  SUMMARY: Describes the ordeal of three teenagers who set out to climb to the summit of Oregon's Mount Hood and encounter snowstorms, an avalanche, and starvation.
    1. Mountaineering — Oregon — Hood, Mount — Juvenile literature. 2. Hood, Mount, Or. — Description — Juvenile literature. [1. Mountaineering. 2. Survival]
  I. Baldini, Tony. II. Title.
  GV199.42.O72H667   796.5'22'0979561   79-22194
  ISBN 0-8172-1552-2 lib. bdg.

CONTENTS

Chapter 1   New Year's Day at 9,000 Feet 7
Chapter 2   Completely Lost 14
Chapter 3   Which Way Are We Going? 22
Chapter 4   An Avalanche, a Storm, a Search 28
Chapter 5   A Clear, Starry Night 35
Chapter 6   Home at Last 42

CHAPTER 1

New Year's Day at 9,000 Feet

"This was a great idea!" Matt Meacham shouted to Gary Schneider and Randy Knapp. "I can't think of a better place to spend New Year's Eve."

"And nobody to slow us down," said Gary. "We'll have the whole mountain to ourselves."

"Right," said Randy. At eighteen, he was two years older than Gary and Matt. "And we couldn't have picked a better day to start our climb."

Randy was right. A strong wind had blown the clouds from the sky. They had a breathtaking view of snowcapped mountains all the way from Mount Jefferson in Oregon to Mount Rainier in Washington. Towering Mount Hood, one of Oregon's most spectacular peaks, stretched out above them.

The boys had started their climb to the top of Mount Hood that morning. They had set out from

7

Timberline Lodge at the base of the mountain. Winter mountaineering is tricky. But the weather was with them, and all three were in good shape. Gary was an expert snow camper. He loved the outdoors. Almost as soon as he could walk, his father had put him on skis and taken him camping. Now at sixteen, he knew practically everything there was to know about hiking, climbing, and camping.

"I figure this will be an easy four-day climb," said Gary, "especially if the weather stays like this." He and Randy had climbed to the top of Mount Hood once before, but this was their first winter climb to the peak.

"No reason why it shouldn't ," said Matt cheerfully as he plunged into a ten-foot snowdrift.

"Let's shoot for the shelter at the top of the ski lift," said Randy, pointing up the mountain. "That'll be a good place to bed down for the night."

"Sounds good," agreed Gary and Matt.

They worked their way up the mountain, stopping occasionally to wave to skiers on the lifts and take photographs. By late afternoon they reached the shelter.

"Here we are," announced Gary, pulling off his pack.

"Looks like it's boarded up," said Matt, eyeing the deserted shelter.

Randy shoved the door. "Shut tight," he said. "Can't get in through these windows," he added. "The whole thing's closed up tighter than a drum."

After trying every window and pushing the door, Gary and Matt had to agree. "Wait," said Gary. He was looking up at the second story of the shelter. "Those windows have hinged openings. We should be able to pry one of them open without too much trouble."

"Yeah, but how do we get to it?" asked Matt.

"No problem," said Gary, taking a rope out of his pack. He knotted a loop at one end of the rope. Then he threw it over the roof, letting the loop fall over the chimney. Gary tested the rope. Then he pulled himself up to the second story window.

"This is a lot easier than climbing up a rock," he called down to Matt and Randy. He worked the window open with his ice ax and let himself in through the window. "Nothing to it," he shouted. "Wait there and I'll open the door from inside."

Once in the shelter, the boys unrolled their sleeping bags and prepared dinner.

"Let's skip New Year's celebrations," yawned Matt as he finished his supper. "I'm beat."

"Going to bed is enough celebration for me," agreed Randy.

They crawled into their sleeping bags and slept until nine the next morning. When they woke up it was bitter cold, but clear and bright.

"What's our elevation?" Matt asked Randy. Randy was studying their map of the mountain.

"We're at 7,000 feet," Randy answered. "And above 9,000 feet it's going to get real steep."

"Then we had better get started," said Gary.

They trudged slowly up the mountainside. Their packs were heavy. And it took them most of the morning to go 2,000 feet.

"You weren't kidding when you said steep," puffed Matt once they passed 9,000 feet. "I feel like I'm walking straight up a wall!"

"Not quite," Gary laughed. "I'd say this slope's about thirty degrees." He stopped. "I don't think we're going to get much farther today. We should begin to think about a shelter for the night."

"You're right. The sun's starting to go down," said Randy looking toward the Pacific Ocean. "What about carving an ice cave? We can slice one right out of the side of this slope."

"I think that's our best bet," agreed Gary. "We're really on too much of an angle to pitch the tent."

"I've never built an ice cave," said Matt. "Is this a good place for one?"

"Practically perfect," said Randy. "We'll just carve a little tunnel for the opening. Then we'll hollow out an area big enough to sleep in."

They began to chip away at the ice and snow with their ice axes. An ice ax is pointed at one end and has a blade on the other. It is one piece of gear no snow camper would be without.

"Does this slope have a name?" asked Matt as they carved into the mountain.

"Illumination Saddle," said Gary, digging deeper into the mountain. "It should take us one day to reach the summit from here."

The boys worked on the cave for over an hour. They dug right into the side of the slope, chipping away until they hollowed out an area they could sleep in. Finally they finished. And it was

beautiful. The cave was eight-feet square, more than big enough for the three of them. They even carved shelves to put their gear on. They knew it would hold. They had carved right into the hard ice and packed snow on the side of the mountain.

"Now this is what I call luxury," sighed Matt as they bedded down for their second night on Mount Hood.

Completely Lost

"This is the route I've mapped out," said Randy the next morning. "We'll go across Reid Glacier then head up the Hour Glass Pass to the top of the mountain. We'll pitch our tent on the summit and spend the night there."

"That'll be a good climb," agreed Gary. "Let's go."

"I didn't figure on these waist-high drifts," said Randy a few hours later. "This soft snow makes it slow going."

"It's taken us most of the morning just to cross this glacier," said Matt. "Will we be able to get up the Hour Glass by sundown?"

"I don't know," Gary said honestly. "A lot will depend on the surface of the pass—whether it's snow-covered or just ice."

After another hour of wading through deep snow they reached the Hour Glass. The narrow pass gleamed with ice. All the snow had been swept away by the wind.

"This won't be easy," said Gary, looking up at the steep, slippery wall of ice. "We'll have to zigzag across the pass. It will be impossible to go straight up."

"We'd better put on our crampons," said Randy. They pulled the spiked metal frames from their packs and strapped them on their boots. These climbing irons make it easier to walk on ice or hard snow.

Using their ice axes to cut holds in the ice, the three slowly made their way across and up the icy slope. They worked steadily, but made discouragingly little progress. After an hour they took a rest stop.

"I just don't have enough ice-climbing experi-

ence," said Matt. "This is real tough going for me. And I'm slowing you down."

"Matt, it's not easy for me, either," said Randy, "and I've done more of this than you have."

Matt and Randy turned to Gary, the most experienced ice-climber of the three. "What do you think we should do?" asked Randy.

Gary shook his head. "We're not going to make it to the top before dark," he said. "It's just too icy. I think we should head back to our cave on Illumination Saddle. Then we can take an easier route to the top tomorrow."

They returned to the cave. By the time they got there it was almost dark. Over a dinner of soup and spaghetti, they mapped out their route for the next day.

"I think we should take the Hogsback trail," decided Randy. He was studying the map by the light of their camping stove. "It's easier, more direct."

"Yes, that's the route we took when you and I climbed the mountain before," agreed Gary. "It's a lot less difficult. We're a day behind schedule, but it's worth trying again. The view from the top is one of the most spectacular sights I've ever seen."

"And when we finally get there, we'll have it all to ourselves," added Matt. "There's no one else on the mountain."

But as they slept a storm gathered. By morning the mountain was covered with new snow. It was still snowing heavily when they woke up.

"I can't see more than thirty yards ahead of me," announced Matt as he looked out into the foggy storm. "I guess we can forget about getting to the top of the mountain."

"The question is whether we should go anywhere in these conditions," said Gary worriedly. "It's dangerous to travel in this kind of whiteout."

"Isn't Timberline Lodge almost directly below us?" asked Randy. "If we go straight down the mountain we should be okay."

"Maybe you're right," Gary agreed. "And there's no way to know how long this storm is going to last." He looked at the swirling snow. "It doesn't look like it's going to blow over very soon. We'll just go slowly and be real careful."

They packed their gear and started carefully down the mountain. Within an hour the storm had become so bad they could see no more than thirty feet ahead.

"It's impossible to see where we're going," said Matt. "I can't get my bearings."

"I can't, either," admitted Gary. "I'm not at all sure we're going straight down the mountain."

"I think we drifted to the side a little, but I'm not positive," said Randy. "It seems to me the lodge is in more of a southeasterly direction."

"I just don't know," said Gary. The strong winds whipped the snow around them. It was difficult for them to hear, or even see, each other.

"The most important thing," Randy shouted over the howl of the storm, "is not to get sepa-

rated. It would be impossible to find each other in this storm."

"You're right," called Gary. "We'd better link arms and head down the mountain side by side."

"If we only knew for sure which way was down," said Matt.

"I think we should go this way," said Randy, pointing in a southeasterly direction.

Arm-in-arm the three boys walked slowly through the blizzard. They had no way of knowing if they were going toward the lodge. They might be straying toward another, unknown part of the mountain. They pushed on as the storm raged around them. Then suddenly, all three fell forward into a crevasse!

Randy was the first to find his feet. "Is everyone

all right?" he shouted anxiously. "Matt, Gary—are you okay?"

"I'm fine," called Matt as he struggled to his feet. "Gary?"

"Over here," he answered, righting himself. "Let's get out of this hole!"

Randy pulled himself out of the crevasse, then reached down to help Matt and Gary.

"We were lucky," Gary said as they sat and rested in the snow. "That crevasse was only waist deep."

"But you know what this means," said Randy. "We've overshot our mark. We must be at the White River Glacier!"

"Yes," said Gary soberly. "The next crevasse

could be hundreds of feet deep. We've gone too far east."

"Let's rope up and head west," said Randy.

They tied the rope around their waists and started off. But the farther they walked, the more anxious they became.

"Does this area look familiar to anyone?" asked Matt.

"No," said Randy quietly, "not at all."

"I don't think this is the mountain above Timberline," said Gary. "The terrain features are different. The land does not look the same."

"In other words," Matt said grimly, "we're completely lost!"

Which Way Are We Going?

"It's too dangerous to keep moving," said Randy. "As long as this storm keeps up, we'll be traveling blind."

"This glacier could be full of crevasses," added Gary. "And I don't want to take any chances of falling into one."

"I guess we should stay here and wait out the storm," Matt suggested. "We may be lost, but we should be safe enough if we don't go anywhere."

"It seems to be our only choice," Gary agreed. "Let's dig out a snow cave and pray the storm ends soon."

Randy looked around him. "There's not enough of a slope to carve a cave into the mountain. We'll have to dig down into the snow. It won't be as secure as our other cave, but it will give us some shelter."

The boys put down their packs and started digging into the snow. The wind blew the falling snow into their faces as they worked.

Matt had dug down three feet when his small aluminum shovel suddenly hit ice. "Stop digging!" he called to Randy and Gary. "It's solid ice down here."

"Maybe we'll have better luck over there!" called Gary, pointing to an area a dozen yards away.

"They moved the dozen yards and started all over again. "Thwack!" Once again Matt's shovel hit ice.

"It's no good," said Gary tiredly. "The whole area must be a bed of solid ice."

"We'll have to pitch the tent," decided Randy.

"The tent won't be much shelter in a storm like this. I'm not even sure it'll hold," Gary pointed out. "Still, it's our only choice at this point."

They began the long hard job of leveling the snow. For two hours they shoveled and packed

the snow down. Finally they had ground firm enough to pitch the tent on.

"I'm soaked through." Matt's teeth chattered as he crawled into the tent.

All three sat around the pole in the center of the tent. They were shivering in their wet clothes.

"Wait a minute," Gary said suddenly. "Do you hear something?"

"Yes," Randy said after a short pause. "It sounds like there's a snow tractor out there somewhere."

"But where?" asked Matt. "It's impossible to tell where the sound is coming from."

"That's because of the storm," Gary explained. "In these conditions, sounds don't seem to have any direction."

"But if there's a tractor out there, we can't be too far from the lodge," said Matt.

"Maybe not," Randy agreed. "But if we tried to follow the sound of the tractor, we could end up on the other side of the mountain."

"He's right, Matt," said Gary. "A snowstorm like this does tricky things to all noises. Our best bet is to sit tight."

Snow continued to pile up throughout the night. The collected snow began to drift against the tent. When they woke up the next morning, the center pole was bent way over from the piled-up snow.

Matt looked out the tent flap. "We must have had over a foot of snow last night," he said.

"If it keeps on like this, I figure we'll get about three feet of snow a day," said Gary. "The tent will never hold."

"It's close to collapsing now," added Randy as he tried to straighten out the center pole.

"I think we should move to a place where we can build an ice cave," said Gary. He had been silently running through their choices. "A cave will offer a lot more shelter. It will keep us warmer and stand more stress than the tent."

"What should we do with the tent?" asked Matt.

"Leave it," Randy answered. "It'll only weigh us down if we take it with us. And the first thing we have to do is find a spot to build a cave. We don't know how far we'll have to travel for that."

They gathered up their gear and loaded their packs. They could hear snowmobiles somewhere out on the mountain.

"I still can't get a fix on where the sound is coming from," said Randy. He listened hard to the faraway noise.

"Me either," said Gary, shaking his head. "But I think we should continue to head west. The last thing we were sure of was that we were too far east."

"Okay, let's go," said Matt as he put on his pack.

They struck out toward the west. The storm still showed no signs of letting up. Wind and snow whirled around them as they fought against the storm.

"The important thing is not to panic," Gary thought to himself. He had learned from his father that an emergency called for a cool head. Gary's father taught skiing and mountaineering at a college nearby. Gary remembered the lecture his father gave new students each year: "A good mountaineer must have steady nerves, emotional strength, physical determination, coolness, courage, and team spirit."

Suddenly, a muffled sound broke in on Gary's thoughts. It sounded like distant thunder. But Gary knew immediately what it was. He had heard it before.

"Brace yourselves!" he shouted to Matt and Randy. "It's an avalanche!"

An Avalanche, a Storm, a Search

The three boys froze. With a mighty roar, a giant wall of snow and ice rumbled by. It swept away everything in its path. Gary looked down at his feet. He was horrified to see that the deep snow ended inches away from his boots. He had been just one step from being carried away by the powerful avalanche.

Only 100 feet away the avalanche disappeared suddenly over a ledge. Gary shivered. "Do you realize how close we slept to that drop-off?" he asked Matt and Randy.

Matt and Randy were both still shaken by the brush with the avalanche.

"I think we should backtrack," said Randy. "At least we know what's back there! Surprises like dropping over a ledge we don't need!"

Gary and Matt agreed. The three boys started back in the direction they had come from. But a soupy, snowy fog closed around them tightly. It

was hard to know if they were going the right way. Snow blew into their faces and the wild storm winds whistled around them.

They moved slowly through the storm. Soon they found themselves walking up a sixty-degree slope.

"Lost again," said Matt. It was hard to keep the discouragement out of his voice.

"I don't think we can go much farther," said Randy. "It's hard to stand on an angle like this, much less walk up it."

"Time to build a snow cave," Gary decided. "At least we have enough of a slope to carve one into the the mountain."

They began to dig out a cave. It was an exhausting effort. They were tired from their battle against the storm. Finally they finished. Randy was moving his equipment in when the cave started to give way.

"The snow's too wet," said Gary as he watched their last hour's work cave in. "Too much weight for the roof to hold."

"Should we even bother to try another one?" asked Matt.

"We have to have shelter," Randy said. "A much smaller cave might hold."

Once again they picked up their equipment and set to work. The new, smaller cave was more secure. It was barely big enough for the three of them, though. There wasn't even enough room for them to sit up. They dragged their sleeping bags into the cave, but left their gear outside. It was that small.

Worn-out, cold, and wet, they turned in for the night.

Matt woke up around midnight. It took him a few minutes to realize that something was not quite right. Then he knew what it was. There wasn't enough oxygen! The falling snow had sealed off the entrance to the cave.

Matt crawled to the cave's entrance. He began to dig away the collected snow that was blocking off their oxygen. The welcome fresh air poured in.

"What a miserable night," he thought to himself as he made his way back to his sleeping bag. "The storm has to end soon," he comforted himself. "How much longer can it last?"

The next morning was their sixth day on the mountain. Snow was falling as fast and hard as it had the first day of the storm. For the next three days, their lives fell into a grim routine as they waited for the storm to let up.

Keeping the cave opening free of snow was the most important, and constant, job. Several times a day, and even during the night, they would shovel the collected snow away from the front of the cave. The tunnel grew longer and longer. They chipped away the ice and packed down the snow to keep the tunnel roof from falling in. The cave began to look like an igloo. Little by little, they made it longer. Now they were a little less cramped when they slept. They even built a bathroom near the main cave.

Except for these tasks, there was little to do but sit and talk. And wait. The storm continued without letup. Each morning there was at least a foot of new snow to greet them.

Days were boring. But nights were even worse. They had made the cave bigger, but it still was not large enough for them to sleep comfortably. Their muscles ached from their awkward positions and the unending cold. There was no way for their sleeping bags to dry out. The wet filling bunched together in lumps.

Their clothes were wool, which was lucky. Even when it's wet, wool provides some insulation from the cold. Clothes made from synthetics wouldn't have given them nearly as much protection against the cold and snow.

For food they had instant puddings, biscuits, dried fruit, and pancake mix. Since they expected the storm to end any day, they didn't really ration their store of food.

"The storm *can't* last much longer," said Randy. It was their ninth day on the mountain.

The three boys sat bunched together in the cave. They nibbled on their lunch—a biscuit and some dried apples.

"There must be a search party looking for us," said Matt. "We were supposed to be back five days ago."

"And our car is still in the lodge parking lot,"

added Randy. "So they'll know we're still up here on the mountain, caught in this storm."

"My father has helped look for lost hikers before," said Gary. "I'm sure he has already made up a search party. If we can just hold out, someone's sure to find us soon. I don't think we're too far from the lodge."

Even as they sat and talked about it, a search party, led by Gary's father, was out in the storm. Mr. Schneider knew the route they had planned to take to the top of Mount Hood. The searchers were prepared for the storm. They had little trouble following the same path the boys had taken. The party finally reached Illumination Saddle, where Gary, Randy, and Matt had built their first ice cave.

But by the time they found it, the cave was covered with snow. Mr. Schneider could not keep the worry out of his voice as he looked at it. "No one has been in this cave for days," he said, looking to the pile of snow blocking the opening. "They could be anywhere on this mountain."

The searchers decided to look farther up the mountain and then continue looking closer to the lodge.

"We'll keep hunting until we find them," said Gary's father.

But no one in the search party was very hopeful.

CHAPTER 5

A Clear, Starry Night

It was their tenth morning on the mountain. Randy was the first to wake up. He picked up the shovel and crawled through the tunnel, now more than twenty feet long, to clear the snow away from the entrance. When he had shoveled his way to the outside, he stopped suddenly. Then he shouted to Matt and Gary, "I can see! Wake up! The storm's clearing!"

Gary and Matt crept quickly to the cave's entrance. The snow had stopped falling! For the first time in eight days there was enough visibility for them to make a safe hike down the mountain. They could see at least 200 yards ahead of them.

"Say goodbye to the cave!" Matt shouted happily. He stretched his legs, thinking ahead to the hike down the mountain. "Today's the day we leave Mount Hood."

"Hey," yelled Gary. "I hear a helicopter."

The sky was cloud-covered. But somewhere

above them was the whirring sound that only helicopter blades make.

"Those clouds are going to lift any minute now," called Randy. "That copter'll see us, and we'll be at the lodge in time for breakfast."

But almost as soon as he finished speaking, the fog closed down around them. Heavy, wet snowflakes began to fall. Too unhappy to say a word, the three boys just stood there. Then they crawled slowly, silently back into the cave.

"Well," said Gary after a few minutes. "I think the time has come to face facts. No matter how unpleasant they may be. Between us, we know a fair amount about snow camping. And I think we've done all the right things so far." He paused for a minute. "But," he continued, "if this storm keeps up, all the skills in the world won't help us. We could die right here in this cave."

Randy and Matt sat quietly, letting Gary's words sink in. They knew he was right. If they were going to live through this, they had to face the danger of their position. Hoping the storm would end soon wouldn't keep them alive. They could no longer turn aside the thought each had been trying to push out of his mind in the last few days. What if the storm didn't end soon?

"Should we try for the lodge again?" asked Matt at last.

"Too risky," said Gary. "We were just lucky

before. The crevasse we fell into was only waist deep. That time it was the avalanche, not us, that fell over that cliff. It would be suicide to go out there in these conditions. I don't like just sitting here any more than you do. But I think it's our best chance for survival. And we all want to live."

"What about the food?" asked Randy. "We're going to have to start rationing what's left." He put their remaining store of food on his sleeping bag in front of him. "Not much here," he said. They had five servings of pancake batter, five packages of pudding mix, and one packet of soup mix.

"The fuel situation's not much better," added Gary as he checked the stove. "About a fourth cup of gas. That'll just barely heat a gallon of water."

Their spirits could not have been lower.

That night, although Randy was against it, Matt and Gary decided to cook up the entire package of soup for dinner. Gary felt they really needed the lift a good meal would give them.

As they finished the last drop of soup, Randy gave in. He agreed that it had been a good idea. "I feel more hopeful already," he smiled.

"And there's enough gas left to melt some snow into drinking water," added Gary. They were able to get four and a half gallons, enough water to hold them for days, if necessary.

"Look," said Matt a few minutes later. "I'm a little worried about this cave. The weight on the roof must be tremendous. We're over twenty feet from the entrance. Do you think it's safe?"

"Maybe we should build a new one," agreed Gary. "We don't want to take any chances of being buried."

They carved out a new cave that night and moved in. Worn-out, they fell asleep immediately.

An odd creaking sound woke them the next morning.

"What's that?" Matt asked sleepily.

The cave groaned again. With a start, Gary sat up in his sleeping bag. "Look out!" he shouted.

"The cave's giving way!" Before they could move, the cave began to collapse. Snow fell down on them as they struggled to pull themselves and their gear out of the cave.

Randy shook his head wearily. "I don't have the strength to build another one," he said as they sat staring at the ruins of the cave.

Neither did Gary or Matt. They decided to move back into the cave they had deserted the night before.

"Let's pray it holds," Gary said somberly. Matt and Randy nodded. They had been thinking the same thing.

Day after dreary snow-filled day passed. At first, the boys tried to keep their spirits up by singing. Not only did the songs make them feel better, but there was also a chance that someone might hear them. But as the hours ticked by the boys got weaker and weaker. Soon they had only enough energy to lie on their sleeping bags and wait for the storm to end.

Food became a critical problem. By their fourteenth day on the mountain, they were eating only one meal a day. That "meal" was two spoonfuls of pancake batter apiece.

Other worries were frostbite and hypothermia. Hypothermia means the body temperature goes down to below ninety degrees. If this happens, the person becomes sleepy and can't think clearly. People with hypothermia are often lulled into a false sense of security. They dazedly think everything is all right. Actually they could be close to death but not take the proper steps to save themselves. Very often victims of hypothermia drop off to sleep and simply never wake up. But the boys were on guard against it.

Gary also made Matt and Randy wiggle their toes constantly to help prevent frostbite. Wiggling movements keep the circulation going, which is important in avoiding frostbite.

"Never give up hope. Survival is all a matter of not becoming panicky," Gary told Matt and Randy over and over again. They were determined not to give up. If they were to stay alive, they knew that believing they would make it was as important as shelter and having enough to eat.

It had stormed for fourteen days. They had been on the mountain for sixteen. That night Matt crawled to the tunnel opening. He started to shovel away the snow. There was less snow blocking the tunnel than usual. He shoveled more quickly. When the entrance was finally clear, he looked out. Matt hardly dared believe what he saw. Above him was a clear, starry night. Below were the lights from Timberline Lodge!

CHAPTER 6

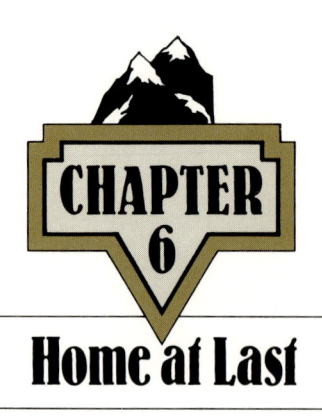

Home at Last

"Should we start down right now?" asked Randy. They were sitting outside the cave, looking down at the lodge.

"I think we should wait until morning," said Gary. "We're in no condition to go hiking in the dark. Besides, I think the storm is really over. There's not a cloud in the sky."

They looked up at the stars. It was the first time in two weeks they had seen them.

When they woke up the next morning, it was a beautiful, blue-skied day. Matt widened the tunnel so they would be able to get their gear out. By this time, the tunnel was easily thirty feet long. As Matt worked on the tunnel, Randy and Gary packed up the equipment.

It took them a while to drag their packs out through the tunnel. But at last they were out. They were ready to start down the mountain.

"I can't believe it was so close for all that time," said Randy as he looked down at Timberline

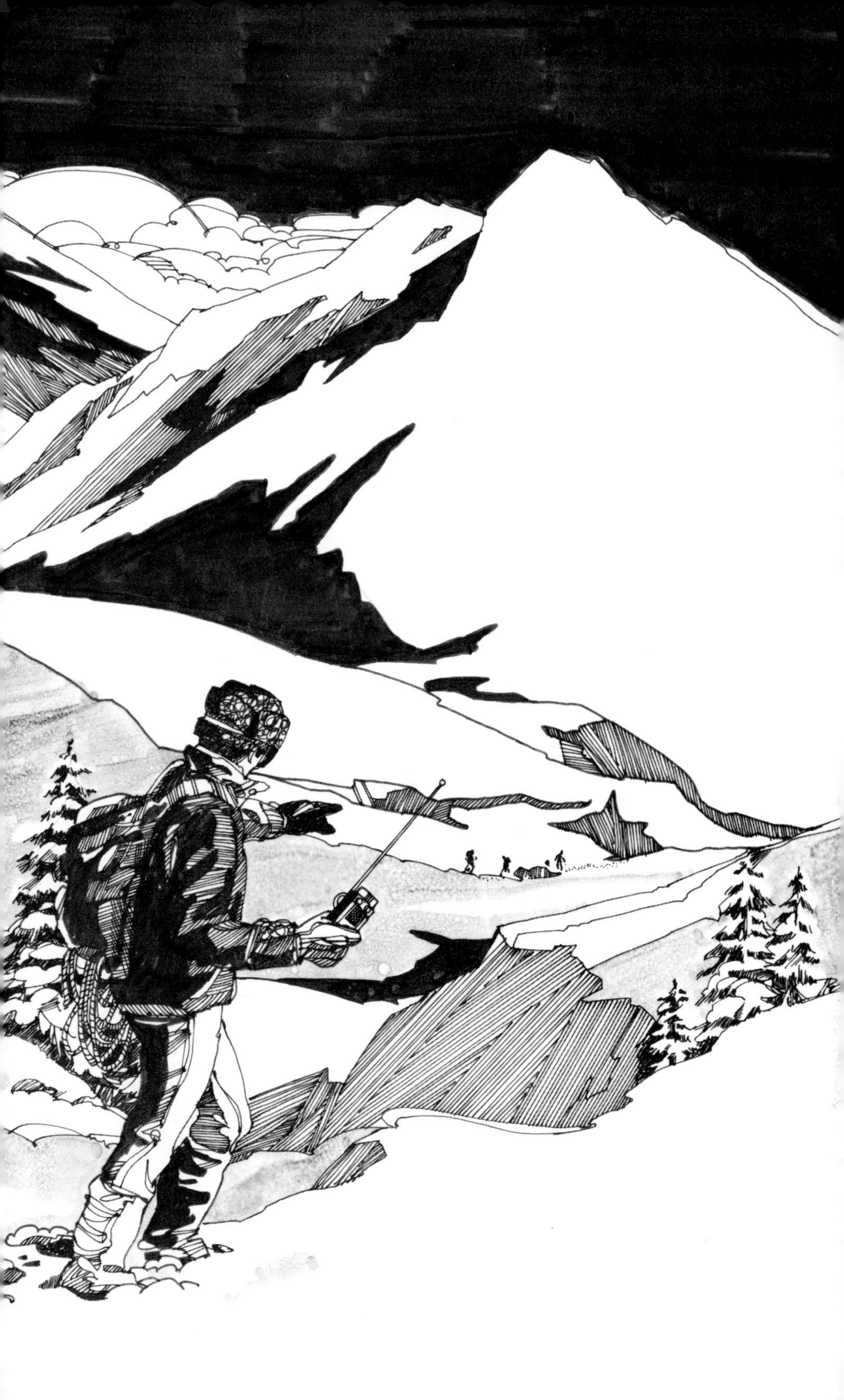

Lodge. His face and voice were filled with wonder. The lodge was no more than 2,000 feet below them.

They started slowly down the mountain, but were only able to go five steps at a time before stopping to rest.

"We're so weak," exclaimed Matt. "It'll take us all day to get down the mountain at this rate."

Meanwhile, Gary's father was about 1,000 feet above them with a search party. Mr. Schneider let out a shout of joy when he sighted the boys. He began running toward them down the mountain.

After a few hundred feet he stopped, realizing there were other searchers on the mountain closer to the boys. He radioed Dave Paulsen, another searcher who was looking for the boys in a Sno-Cat. "They're about 2,000 feet directly north of the lodge," Gary's father said over his walkie-talkie. "You can reach them in a matter of minutes."

"I'm on my way," said Paulsen. He put the Sno-Cat into gear and charged across the mountain.

When he found the boys, Paulsen burst into tears of relief. He hugged all three. "I can't believe it," he said over and over again. "Your father never gave up hope," he said to Gary as he began to lift their packs into the tractor. The packs were so soaked with water that they each weighed about eighty-five pounds. "He had a lot of faith in the three of you," he added.

The boys climbed into the Sno-Cat and rode the 2,000 feet down to the lodge. Crowds of skiers gathered around. Everyone knew that a search had been underway for three boys trapped on the mountain. A huge cheer went up when the Sno-Cat reached the lodge and the skiers realized the lost boys were in the tractor.

A doctor was on hand. He looked them over quickly and then rushed them to a nearby hospital for a complete checkup.

The boys had survived for two weeks, through one of Mount Hood's worst storms. The longest anyone had survived a Mount Hood storm before had been five days. And in that group, one of the three climbers had died.

Matt, Gary, and Randy were sent home from the hospital three days later. Each of them had lost about twenty-five pounds, but, on the whole, they were in good shape. Matt had a touch of frostbite, but it was nothing serious. Within a week and a half, all three were back in school.

They had lived, experts decided, because their training was good and because they didn't give up. Many people die in storms because they give up hope and stop fighting to stay alive.

One year later, almost to the day, Gary and Randy climbed Mount Hood again. They made it to the top and back down with no problems.